WORLD STUDIES

EUROPE

by Clara MacCarald

FOCUS
READERS®

VOYAGER

www.focusreaders.com

Focus Readers is distributed by North Star Editions:
sales@northstareditions.com | 888-417-0195

Produced for Focus Readers by Red Line Editorial.

Content Consultant: Kristin Rebien, PhD, Associate Professor of German and European Studies, San Diego State University

Photographs ©: Shutterstock Images, cover, 1, 4–5, 7, 8–9, 13, 19, 20–21, 23, 24, 27, 28–29, 31; iStockphoto, 11, 14–15, 17; Frank Augstein/AP Images, 33; Monika Skolimowska/picture-alliance/dpa/AP Images, 34–35; Yves Herman/Reuters/AP Images, 37; Red Line Editorial, 39; Brian Lawless/PA Wire URN:34748279/Press Association/AP Images, 40–41; Kiran Ridley/Getty Images News/Getty Images, 43; Vaclav Salek/CTK/AP Images, 44

Library of Congress Cataloging-in-Publication Data
Names: MacCarald, Clara, 1979- author.
Title: Europe / by Clara MacCarald.
Description: Lake Elmo, MN : Focus Readers, [2021] | Series: World studies | Includes index. | Audience: Grades 7-9
Identifiers: LCCN 2020011112 (print) | LCCN 2020011113 (ebook) | ISBN 9781644933992 (hardcover) | ISBN 9781644934753 (paperback) | ISBN 9781644936276 (pdf) | ISBN 9781644935514 (ebook)
Subjects: LCSH: Europe--History--Juvenile literature. | Europe--Geography--Juvenile literature.
Classification: LCC D1051 .M29 2021 (print) | LCC D1051 (ebook) | DDC 940--dc23
LC record available at https://lccn.loc.gov/2020011112
LC ebook record available at https://lccn.loc.gov/2020011113

Printed in the United States of America
Mankato, MN
012021

ABOUT THE AUTHOR

Clara MacCarald is a freelance writer with a master's degree in biology. She lives with her family in an off-grid house nestled in the forests of central New York. When not parenting her daughter, she spends her time writing nonfiction books for kids.

TABLE OF CONTENTS

CHAPTER 1

WELCOME TO EUROPE

Europe is a land of towering mountains and peaceful valleys. Traces of history can be seen in grand castles, ancient ruins, and even city streets. Europe is also famous for its local food traditions, art museums, music halls, and more.

Europe is the world's second-smallest continent. It is part of the supercontinent Eurasia. Mainland Europe stretches from Spain and Portugal in the west to Russia in the east.

London, England, has been one of Europe's most populated cities for hundreds of years.

Europe contains approximately 50 countries. Some, such as Russia, also include land in Asia. Many island-nations are also in Europe, such as Iceland and the United Kingdom (UK). The British city of London is important in culture and finance.

Experts often divide Europe into four regions. These are Western Europe, Eastern Europe, Northern Europe, and Southern Europe. Spain and Italy are two major countries of Southern Europe. Rome, Italy, was once the center of a vast empire. France and Germany are in Western Europe. Paris, France, has been a center of culture since medieval times. Berlin, Germany, is a place where Western and Eastern Europe have come together.

Russia, Poland, and Romania are in Eastern Europe. More than 12 million people live in Moscow, Russia. This city is also Russia's capital. Major Northern European countries include

Sweden, Norway, and Finland. These countries have hundreds of thousands of islands. European countries are rich with history and culture.

REGIONS OF EUROPE

NORTHERN EUROPE
WESTERN EUROPE
EASTERN EUROPE
SOUTHERN EUROPE

CHAPTER 2

HISTORY OF EUROPE

Humans have lived in Europe for more than 40,000 years. Early hunter-gatherers lived in small groups. They used stone tools and made art with natural materials. Approximately 8,000 years ago, people brought farming to Europe. These people came from the Middle East. Over time, some groups became more complex. In 3200 BCE, for example, ancient Greece became a center of culture and trade.

The Acropolis in Athens was a cultural center of ancient Greece. Its ruins still stand today.

Europe became more connected under the Roman Empire. By 117 CE, the empire's rule stretched from the Middle East to what is now the UK. The Romans built vast road systems. They spread technologies such as sewer systems and concrete. In 323 CE, the empire became Christian.

The Roman Empire's unity did not last. By 476 CE, it had lost Western and Southern Europe. Local rulers rose to power there. The Catholic Church became powerful in those regions. In Eastern Europe, however, the Roman Empire kept control. A different type of Christianity developed there. It became known as Eastern Orthodoxy.

At the same time, Jewish communities lived across Europe. And in the 710s, a Muslim army conquered Spain. In addition, the Vikings raided, traded, and settled along Europe's coasts and rivers. These Scandinavian people were **pagan**.

▲ Opened in 80 CE, the Colosseum provided entertainment to huge crowds during the Roman Empire.

Europeans began to look more to the outside world. In 1095, the Catholic Church ordered an army to invade parts of the Middle East. These wars were known as the Crusades. Trade with other regions also increased during this time. In the 1300s, the **Renaissance** began. Knowledge, science, and culture spread throughout Europe.

Powerful groups struggled for power. Cities by the Baltic Sea formed the Hanseatic League. This league controlled trade across Northern Europe.

The Ottoman Empire formed in approximately 1300. Over time, it expanded into Eastern Europe. The empire was opposed by a line of rulers known as the Habsburgs. In the 1400s, Russia took over new territories as well. It grew to a great size.

Many countries kept exploring. Portugal and Spain sailed ships around the world. France and England followed suit. Over hundreds of years, European countries **colonized** most of the world. These countries enslaved and killed millions of **Indigenous** people. They also captured millions of people in Africa. Traders brought African people to the Americas and sold them into slavery.

The **Industrial Revolution** brought more major changes. Starting in the 1700s, cities and industries grew rapidly. Many people could afford more goods. New methods of travel, such as trains, had society on the move.

Germany's invasion of Poland in September 1939 marked the beginning of World War II.

Militaries also used this industrial technology. During World War I (1914–1918), European countries fought against one another in the first modern war. They fought again in World War II (1939–1945). These wars killed tens of millions of people. Many countries were devastated.

After World War II, many former colonies of Europe gained independence. At the same time, the **Cold War** pitted Western Europe against Eastern Europe. After the Cold War, the European Union (EU) formed. This organization joined many European countries together.

CHAPTER 3

GEOGRAPHY AND CLIMATE

To the far north, Europe meets the Arctic Ocean. Countries such as Norway and Iceland border this ocean. Their coasts feature jagged cliffs and long inlets called fjords. In places such as Finland and northern Russia, winters can be very cold and snowy. In contrast, much of Western Europe enjoys mild temperatures and plenty of rain. Western Europe is still fairly far north. But the region is warmer than other northern areas.

In parts of Northern Europe such as Iceland, people can see the northern lights.

A current in the Atlantic Ocean brings heat up from the equator. This current creates Western Europe's pleasant climate.

Some regions of Eastern Europe have continental climates. These regions experience more extreme seasons. Rain is also limited. At the same time, Europe's southern coasts have Mediterranean climates. Similar to Eastern Europe, summers here are often hot and dry. But the winters tend to be mild and wet.

Large plains stretch from France to Russia. Several mountain chains also cross mainland Europe. The Pyrenees separate France from Spain. The Alps arc through France, Switzerland, Austria, and northern Italy. Snowfall can be very heavy in mountain areas.

A few major rivers also run through Europe. The Danube River flows for more than 1,770 miles

⚠ Many cities, including Rybinsk in Russia, lie along the Volga River.

(2,850 km). It stretches from Germany's Black Forest to the Black Sea. The longest European river is the Volga River. The Volga runs for 2,193 miles (3,530 km). It starts near Moscow, Russia. It flows all the way to the Caspian Sea.

Climate change is affecting all parts of Europe. Average temperatures across Europe are rising. Glaciers are shrinking in the mountains. In 2019, summer heat waves broke temperature records across Europe. As this crisis increases, all forms of life will need to adapt to survive.

THE ALPS

The Alps are a chain of mountains located in Southern and Western Europe. The Alps stretch approximately 750 miles (1,200 km). They reach from France to Austria. The highest peak is Mont Blanc. This mountain towers 15,771 feet (4,800 m) above sea level.

Approximately 30,000 animal species make their homes in the Alps. Native animals include alpine salamanders, brown bears, and bearded vultures. In addition, thousands of plant species grow in the Alps. Near mountain peaks, plants are exposed to high winds and extreme temperatures. The soil also tends to be poor. However, some plants have adapted to handle the soil and harsh weather. Native flowers include edelweiss and alpenrose.

The Alps are popular with humans as well. More than 11 million people live in the Alps.

▲ Mont Blanc is split between France, Italy, and Switzerland.

Approximately 120 million tourists visit every year. Many come to ski. Tourists also explore mountain trails on foot or on bikes. Climbers tackle the high peaks. Visitors sample local culture and visit historic sites such as castles.

The Alps hold thousands of glaciers. These glaciers bring many tourists to the area. They also provide water to all kinds of life. However, rising temperatures have caused these glaciers to shrink. As the ice melts, plants, animals, and people will have to adapt to a new environment.

CHAPTER 4

PLANTS AND ANIMALS

Europe contains a wide range of ecosystems. Even the cold waters of the far north are full of life. Swarms of tiny creatures known as plankton float in the ocean. The plankton feed larger animals such as crabs, sponges, and bowhead whales. Underwater forests of seaweed provide breeding grounds for fish. Fish provide food for predators such as seabirds, seals, and beluga whales. Polar bears hunt seals on the ice.

Many people visit Svalbard, Norway, to go on polar bear tours.

The tundra covers parts of northern countries such as Russia and Iceland. Mosses, lichens, and ferns grow on this treeless plain. Reindeer roam over its frozen ground. Arctic foxes hunt small animals. The foxes also feed on dead animals left by wolves and polar bears.

Evergreen forests lie south of the tundra. Northern forests and wetlands provide habitats for a variety of wildlife. Mammals such as brown bears, moose, and wolverines live there. Huge flocks of birds breed in these areas, too.

Farther south, broad-leaved trees such as oaks and beeches take over. People cleared much of mainland Europe to make room for farming and cities. But forests, grasslands, and wetlands still remain. Birds such as black woodpeckers and hazel grouse live in the forests. The European otter swims through the region's rivers and

The Barbary macaque lives in Gibraltar, a small British territory along the Mediterranean coast.

swamps. There are also several native species of rare amphibians. One example is the cave salamander.

Pine and cork oak trees grow near the Mediterranean Sea. Billions of birds travel through this region every year. The fire salamander is one of many native species found in Southern Europe. Wildlife also includes the only primate native to Europe, the Barbary macaque.

Seaweed and coral grow in the Mediterranean Sea. Hundreds of fish species live there, too. Many live nowhere else in the world. The Egyptian sole, for example, is a flatfish that can only be found in the Mediterranean. Sharks, rays, and whales also swim in the Mediterranean Sea. The fin whale is the second-largest whale on Earth.

Approximately 15 percent of European animals are at risk of dying out. One example is the Balearic shearwater. This bird breeds only on certain islands of Spain. Invasive species and fishing boats have been killing shearwaters. For these reasons, the bird's numbers are plunging. In response, Spain has protected the areas where shearwaters nest.

People have returned some animals to lands where they once roamed. For example, the European bison went extinct in the wild in 1919. People have returned bison to countries such as Poland and the Netherlands. European beavers never died out. But hunting had cut their numbers by the early 1900s. Approximately 1,000 beavers remained in the wild. Since then, people have returned beavers to habitats across Europe.

THINK ABOUT IT ◁

Do you think people should return animals back to the wild? Why or why not?

LYNXES

The Eurasian lynx is Europe's third-largest predator. Only brown bears and wolves are larger. The heaviest Eurasian lynxes weigh approximately 62 pounds (28 kg). But they can kill red deer weighing 485 pounds (220 kg). More often, though, lynxes eat smaller animals such as roe deer or mountain hares.

Approximately 9,000 Eurasian lynxes live in mainland Europe outside of Russia and Belarus. These cats need large stretches of forests filled with prey. But the lynxes can survive in many different climates. Some live in northern evergreen forests. Others live in southern Mediterranean forests. Lynxes can also be found in the Alps.

The Eurasian lynx is not at risk of dying out. However, another kind of lynx is at risk. Iberian lynxes roam the forests of southern Spain. They

▲ Eurasian lynxes are spotted cats that can be 24 inches (60 cm) tall.

hunt rabbits and other prey there. This lynx is the most at-risk wildcat on Earth. In 2015, approximately 400 remained.

Several programs have returned lynxes to parts of Europe where they had died out. People want the wildcats to keep prey populations under control. In some areas, people think lynxes will appeal to tourists. Visitors may want to see the cats in their natural habitat.

CHAPTER 5

NATURAL RESOURCES AND ECONOMY

Europe benefits from many natural resources. Forests provide jobs for millions of Europeans. Trees are made into paper and furniture. Natural cork comes from the bark of the cork oak tree. This tree grows in Mediterranean forests. People also harvest edible mushrooms. One valuable type of mushroom is called a truffle.

European bodies of water help a variety of economies. They support a number of fisheries.

The cork oak tree is the national tree of Portugal.

For example, fishing boats seek bluefin tuna in the warm waters of the Mediterranean Sea. European fishers also have farms for fish and shellfish. Norway and other northern countries raise cod. They use eggs laid by wild fish.

Olive trees and grapevines grow well in the Mediterranean climates of Southern Europe. Italy and Spain are world leaders in olive and grape production. The European plains generally have good soil and climates. For this reason, countries such as France and Ukraine grow vast fields of wheat and corn.

Livestock and livestock-related products are important, too. Europe is famous for its local cheeses and fancy meats. Camembert cheese is made in France. Parmesan cheese comes from Italy. A well-known type of cured ham from Italy is called prosciutto.

▲ Scotland is home to more than 6.5 million sheep.
In fact, Scotland has more sheep than people.

Some countries have important metals and minerals under the ground. For example, Serbia has large amounts of copper. Sweden has iron ores. The EU is a leader in feldspar production. Feldspar is a mineral used in glass and pottery manufacturing. Italy and Norway have rocks such as marble and granite. These rocks are used around the world as building materials.

Deposits of oil and natural gas lie under the North Sea. Other fuel deposits are found under land. There are large oil and gas fields in Russia. Coal lies under the UK and many parts of mainland Europe.

Manufacturing also makes up a large part of many European economies. In general, manufacturing in Western Europe creates expensive goods such as steel and vehicles. Eastern Europe tends to produce less-expensive goods, including cloth and food products.

Service industries are important to Europe as well. These industries include trade, banking, technology, and tourism. Many cities provide business and financial services. London is a global financial capital. Another important financial city is Frankfurt, Germany. Frankfurt is home to the central bank of the entire EU.

▲ Germany has the largest economy in Europe. Germany produces millions of cars every year.

Hundreds of millions of tourists visit Europe every year. Planes fly tourists in. Cruise lines bring people to coastal cities such as Barcelona, Spain, and Venice, Italy. Hotels provide places to stay. Cafés and restaurants provide meals. Tourists also visit natural areas, such as the Alps and Mediterranean beaches.

CHAPTER 6

GOVERNMENT AND POLITICS

Governments in Europe vary by country. But nearly all of them are republics. In a republic, citizens elect many of the representatives who run the country. France and Finland are both republics. Other countries have federal republics. These countries are made up of states. Each state has some power to govern itself. But a federal government leads the group of states. Germany, Switzerland, and Austria are three examples.

A German citizen casts her ballot during Germany's 2017 federal election.

Other countries work much like republics. For example, the UK and Belgium have monarchies. But their monarchs don't control the country. Instead, **parliaments** make most of the laws and rules for Belgium and the UK. Similar to republics, citizens elect most members of these parliaments.

Officially, Russia is another democratic republic. Citizens elect their president. In practice, however, Vladimir Putin has kept a strict hold on the country since becoming president in 2000. His government has cracked down on opposing parties.

Many European nations are wary of Russia. In 2014, Russia seized the Crimean Peninsula from Ukraine. Other countries were alarmed. Russia is also attacking democracies online. Computer users linked to Russia have spread false information. Russia's goal appears to be to

European leaders meet in Brussels, Belgium, in 2020 to discuss the European Union's budget.

influence elections. Russia may want to weaken other European countries. It may be trying to weaken the EU as well.

As of February 2020, the EU was made up of 27 countries. The EU joins these countries together in economic, political, and cultural ways. For instance, 19 EU countries use the same kind of money. This money is known as the euro.

Citizens can move and live freely in any country in the EU. They can also vote in local elections.

EU membership can bring problems, however. The EU limits its countries' ability to control themselves. For example, a global financial crisis hit the EU in 2009. In response, the EU loaned money to countries such as Greece. But the EU also limited how Greece could tax and spend.

In addition, the EU can take legal action against its countries. For example, Hungary and Poland have taken steps to make their presses and justice systems less free. The EU called on Hungary and Poland to reverse their actions.

> # THINK ABOUT IT

What are some reasons that new countries might be interested in joining the EU?

Otherwise, the countries could lose their ability to vote in the EU.

Several countries, such as Albania, are working to join the EU. One country has left. In 2016, people in the UK voted to leave the EU. The act was known as Brexit. Disagreements over the act led to delays. Finally, Brexit happened on January 31, 2020. The UK left the EU. The UK agreed to remain in the EU market until December 31, 2020.

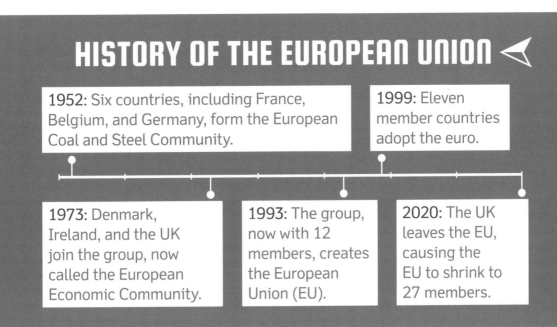

HISTORY OF THE EUROPEAN UNION ◁

1952: Six countries, including France, Belgium, and Germany, form the European Coal and Steel Community.

1999: Eleven member countries adopt the euro.

1973: Denmark, Ireland, and the UK join the group, now called the European Economic Community.

1993: The group, now with 12 members, creates the European Union (EU).

2020: The UK leaves the EU, causing the EU to shrink to 27 members.

CHAPTER 7

PEOPLE AND CULTURE

The people and cultures of Europe are very diverse. In the EU alone, people speak more than 80 different languages. Most EU citizens can chat in at least two languages. Some European languages are also common around the world. These languages include English and Spanish.

Other languages are mostly spoken only in Europe. For instance, more than 1.8 million people throughout Ireland can speak Irish Gaelic.

Students in Northern Ireland protest in support of protecting Irish Gaelic.

Where France and Spain meet, approximately 700,000 people speak Basque. In addition, **immigrants** have brought their own languages from other parts of the world.

Europe has a wide variety of religions. Most Europeans consider themselves Christian. The second-largest group does not follow a religion or does not believe in a god. Tens of millions of Muslims live in Europe. More than one million Europeans are Jewish. Similar numbers are Hindus or Buddhists. Some people follow folk religions.

The continent is home to a variety of rich cultures. For instance, France is known around the world for its food. Meals form an important part of many French communities. The kinds of food vary greatly from place to place. But the French share ways of finding local food, setting the table, and even tasting food and drink.

▲ People in France march against Islamophobia in 2019. France has the largest Muslim population in Europe.

Hungarians have roots from the Magyars. These people have lived in the area since the 800s. Even so, Hungary is always changing. In the 1800s, the Matyó people began making clothing with colorful and complex patterns. This art form represents Hungarian culture to this day.

Some cultural groups do not have a country. The Roma are the largest minority in Europe. Millions of Romani people live throughout Europe.

▲ Girls participate in a Roma Pride march in Brno, Czechia, in 2019.

Instead of a country, family identity often unites Romani people. However, the Roma have faced mistreatment and violence for hundreds of years.

Some cultural groups want independence. Catalonia is a region in Spain. Catalonia has been distinctive for 1,000 years. People speak their own language. The region has its own parliament. In 2017, Catalonia tried to declare itself independent. But Spain quickly took back control of the region. Relations between Catalonia and the Spanish government continue to be tense.

Scotland is part of the UK. But many Scots want to have an independent Scotland. Scots voted against independence in 2014. But after the UK left the EU, the push for independence grew.

Immigrants have come to Europe for thousands of years. In 2015, Europe saw a steep increase in immigrants. People were fleeing conflict in countries such as Syria and Afghanistan. Europe will continue to change as a result of immigration.

THINK ABOUT IT ◄

Consider the history of Europe. Why are some European languages spoken in many places around the world?

FOCUS ON
EUROPE

Write your answers on a separate piece of paper.

1. Write a paragraph describing the main ideas of Chapter 7.

2. Some European cultures are closely connected to the countries they come from. Others are not connected to any country. How are culture and country connected where you live?

3. In 2020, what country left the European Union?

    A. Germany
    B. Albania
    C. the United Kingdom

4. What would happen if the large ocean current flowing from the equator to Europe didn't exist?

    A. European glaciers would melt faster.
    B. Eastern Europe would be warmer than it is now.
    C. Western Europe would be colder than it is now.

Answer key on page 48.

GLOSSARY

climate change
A human-caused global crisis involving long-term changes in Earth's temperature and weather patterns.

Cold War
A conflict of ideals between the United States and the Soviet Union that took place during the second half of the 1900s.

colonized
Established control over an area and the people who live there.

immigrants
People who move to a new country.

Indigenous
Native to a region, or belonging to ancestors who lived in a region before colonists arrived.

Industrial Revolution
Starting in Great Britain in the 1700s, a huge economic shift involving the use of powerful machines and mass production.

pagan
Religious beliefs that are not part of one of the world's major religions.

parliaments
Groups of people who make laws.

Renaissance
A period between the 1300s and 1600s in Europe involving advances in science, culture, and arts.

TO LEARN MORE

BOOKS

Dougherty, Martin J. *The Untold History of the Vikings.* New York: Cavendish Square, 2017.

Sheehan, Sean, and Debbie Nevins. *Romania.* New York: Cavendish Square, 2016.

Voices from the Second World War: Stories of War as Told to Children of Today. Somerville, MA: Candlewick Press, 2018.

NOTE TO EDUCATORS

Visit **www.focusreaders.com** to find lesson plans, activities, links, and other resources related to this title.

INDEX

Answer Key: 1. Answers will vary; **2.** Answers will vary; **3.** C; **4.** C